The Odds

For Caleb and Penny – original pranksters ~ AP

For Joseph ~ TM

STRIPES PUBLISHING
An imprint of Little Tiger Press
1 The Coda Centre, 189 Munster Road,
London SW6 6AW

A paperback original
First published in Great Britain in 2012

Text copyright © Adam Perrott, 2012
Illustrations copyright © Tom McLaughlin, 2012

ISBN: 978-1-84715-251-0

The right of Adam Perrott and Tom McLaughlin to be identified as the
author and illustrator of this work respectively has been asserted by them
in accordance with the Copyright, Designs and Patents Act, 1988.

Printed and bound in the UK.
2 4 6 8 10 9 7 5 3

The Odds

Adam Perrott

Illustrated by
Tom McLaughlin

Stripes

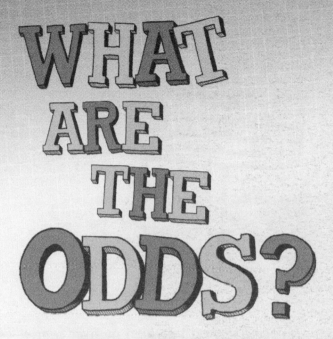

WHAT ARE THE ODDS?

This is a story about Meddlers.

And custard.

But mainly Meddlers.

Before you read on I must warn you, Meddlers are not kindly folk to wrap up warm and snug with on a cold Sunday evening. Oh no. They are a sneaky and slippery type of people. Especially the Odds...

Mr Odd, Mrs Odd, twins Edgar and Elsie Odd, and their Odd dog Bob lived in Trott, a place famous for its custard and tripwire.

Mr and Mrs Odd had arrived in Trott many years earlier, with their flea-bitten mongrel, and had raised a family there. They had moved to the town from Meddleton, the Meddling capital of the world.

The Odds lived at Number 13 Rotten Row. The tall terraced house was pretty much the same as all the other houses around it, only a bit ... *odder*. It was full of damp patches, mould, curtain-lice and carpet-nits, but the oddest thing about it by far was the Odds themselves.

That was because the Odds were Meddlers.

You won't have heard of Meddlers (or Professional Pranksters as those fully qualified in Prankery and Prankification are known). Meddlers are responsible for all the tricky, flicky, throw-a-bag-of-sicky things that happen to us every day. For example, have you ever put down a glass of juice, gone to do something else and when you get back the drink is NOWHERE to be seen?

THAT'S A MEDDLER!

How about when you're walking downstairs and suddenly you miss a step and your insides feel like you've just swallowed a load of giddy squids?

THAT'S A MEDDLER!

And why, when you're walking along minding your own business, holding your 99 ice cream with raspberry sauce, do you always trip up and then...

WHAMMO!

You end up sprawled on the ground covered in raspberry sauce with half a flake up your left nostril? Think about it. Do you ever trip up when you *haven't* got your hands full of ice cream, or  your brand-new hand-held games console, or worse – your mum's prized collection of ceramic hamsters? NO! (Unless, of course, you live in the Trott Tripwire Testing Centre.) Well...

THAT'S A MEDDLER!

And have you ever woken up in the morning and found your whole body covered with itchy red spots?

THAT'S THE CHICKEN POX!

Every village, town and city in the world has at least one Meddling family like the Odds in it.

If you don't happen to live in Trott, then it is highly likely you live near another family of Meddlers – perhaps the Peculiars or the Stranges or the Weirdlys. You never know, Mr Peculiar himself may be stealing your bookmark or rummaging through your sock drawer hiding all your left socks even as you read this.

All Meddlers and Meddling families tend to look alike. If you were to sight a Meddler up close you would see they were about as tall as a medium-sized garden gate. Or half a phone box high. Or a bit taller than the back of a chair. Yet if you looked again they could be sitting comfortably in a plant pot with a geranium on their heads, or be peering out of the slit in a post box. In fact, they can fit into all sorts of places you wouldn't be able to, like drawers or goldfish bowls or wellington boots.

The Odds themselves were a scrawny bunch, who stood with their backs hunched and their shoulders slumped. Edgar and Elsie Odd were smaller than their parents, as most young children tend to be. Edgar's hair was greasy and home to many things not normally found in a boy's hair (woodlice, spare pens, assorted wildlife). Elsie's hair hung in pigtails tied with dried worms.

Mrs Odd wore a dark green tweed dress, stripy purple-and-green tights and black buckled boots. Her wild and witchy hair was scraped back into a bun and held in place with a knife and fork.

Mr Odd always wore a scruffy brown suit with mustard-yellow pinstripes and a wilted dandelion (picked fresh every morning) in his buttonhole. His shirt was originally white, but was now a sort of murky grey. His tie was a dark purple velvet and ended just after the knot. He had snipped it himself in accordance with *The Meddlers' Mischief Manual.*

The Meddlers' Mischief Manual guides all Meddlers on how to be the finest, most fiendish fiddlers they can. It is a huge, ancient book full of Meddling law, hints and tips for pulling off those perfect pranks, a few songs and poems, and some specially selected recipes. Though basically, the entire contents can be whittled down to just seven words:

If it causes mischief, then do it.

Each of the Odds had their own area of pranking expertise, though a skilled Meddler will have skills in many, if not all, types. The Prime Meddler (the Meddler in charge of all other Meddlers) himself has stated:

"A Meddler must meddle masterfully, or mishaps may happen."

Mr Odd enjoyed hiding things – keys, bags, wallets, purses, elderly relatives – especially when the victim looking for them was already running late.

Mrs Odd's special area of prankery was mess and confusion. For example, if someone was walking down the street with lots and lots of shopping bags in their hands, Mrs Odd thought it the funniest thing in the world to trip them up and watch them fall over, spilling their shopping everywhere. Oh, how she'd chuckle as grapefruit and tins of dog food and tuna and Spam went spinning down the pavement, knocking into passing pedestrians.

Boing!

Huh?

The twins were not yet Professional Pranksters, but Trainee Tricksters. However, they still had more tricks up their sleeves than the average magician. They went to the local primary, St Mumps. Like all Meddler children they attended a normal school, but instead of paying attention in Maths and Science and Fishing and Geography like all the other kids, they went solely to practise their pranking.

Edgar was fond of scary pranks and Elsie's speciality was "little accidents". So if there's ever been a power-cut just as you're about to complete the final level of *Killer Jackrabbits From the Planet Furry*, then you trip over in the darkness, it was probably Edgar and Elsie combining forces.

So there we have them. The Odds. Expert Meddlers and no doubt about it. There was no prank the Odds couldn't pull off and no one they couldn't prank.

No way.

No how.

That is, until they met the Plopwells...

Chapter One

BREAKFAST WITH THE ODDS

It was a Monday morning, and Mr Odd, Mrs Odd and the twins were at the breakfast table. The Odds didn't limit their prankery to the poor residents of Trott. Oh no indeedio. They also loved playing tricks on each other, so breakfast with the Odds was a dangerous affair. In fact, almost *everything* to do with the Odds was a dangerous affair.

Mr Odd sat reading Trott's best and only newspaper, *The Daily Week*, whilst sprinkling his usual eighteen-and-a-half spoonfuls of sugar on to his porridge. Mrs Odd was frying some lovely thick rashers of bacon in the kitchen. Edgar and Elsie were dressed in their murky snot-green school jumpers, Edgar in grey shorts and Elsie a grey skirt, munching their cereal and trying not to giggle.

Bob was asleep under the table, which was usually the safest place to be when the Odds were in the same room. In his younger days, he and Mr Odd had been quite the pair of practical pranksters, getting up to all sorts of japes and tricks together. But now Bob was content to enjoy his retirement either sleeping or sitting around, counting his fleas. Still, in his dreams he relived the glory days when he had been an expert pranking pooch. The kind who could piddle a rude word on a Persian rug in a crowded room and be gone before anyone had even noticed.

Mr Odd turned a page and grunted. "Hmph. Says 'ere there's a new fancy-pants pair of money-baggers movin' into Snootypants Manor on Choffingly Way. There's my meddlin' fer the day, I thinks."

"Look!" said Edgar, peering at an advert on the back page of the paper. "It says the circus is in town. Can we go?"

"I don't see why not," said Mr Odd, heaping a huge, sugary spoonful of porridge into his mouth. He chewed once, twice, three times and then swallowed. He was about to eat a second spoonful when he froze. His eyes began to water and his mouth began ... *foaming*. There was a moment's pause before he leaped from his chair and began spitting all over the dining-room floor. Spitting, as I'm sure you know, is a disgusting habit, but to the Odds it was perfectly acceptable. They were, after all, the stinkiest, finkiest, toilet-water-drinkiest family in all of Trott, if not the entire world.

"SOAP!" cried Mr Odd, belching a great big whopper of a soap bubble between spittings. "YOU'VE SWAPPED THE SUGAR FOR SOAP POWDER!"

Elsie collapsed in a heap of giggles, and Edgar laughed so hard the milk from his cereal squirted out of his nose.

You might think that Mr Odd would be angry at his two children for playing such a rotten prank on him first thing in the morning, but he wasn't. He grabbed his glass of nettle juice, drank it all in one great gluggle and smiled at the twins.

"Well done, my little ferret-sniffers!" he beamed. "You've not done the sugar and soap swap since..." He scratched his stubbly chin. "...Ooh, yesterday evening!"

"When you told us to swap them back," said Edgar, rocking on his chair in hysterics, "we didn't!"

"We just pretended!" screeched Elsie, secretly spooning some soap powder on to Edgar's cereal.

"Well, I'm very proud of you both!" said Mr Odd.

At that moment, there was a tremendous scream from the kitchen. Mrs Odd came running into the dining room, waving her frying pan as if she were trying to swat an enormous bluebottle.

"What's going on?" Mr Odd shouted. "Whatever's wrong with you, my little wart-face?" Wart-face was Mr Odd's favourite pet name for his wife, but it certainly wasn't hers. Her favourite was trout-nose.

"CROCODILES!" shrieked Mrs Odd, leaping on to a chair. "CROCODILES IN THE KITCHEN!"

"Crocodiles?" Mr Odd repeated. "Are you sure?"

"Come and see!" cried Mrs Odd, hitching her dress above her knees.

Mr Odd went into the kitchen and, sure enough, there were two small and very greasy baby crocodiles waddling around on the floor, snapping their jaws as they chewed on fallen scraps of bacon.

"It was us, Mum," Elsie guffawed.

"We swapped the normal eggs for some crocodile eggs we've been saving!" Edgar sniggered.

Mrs Odd looked at her children. Her expression changed from one of horror and surprise to one of deepest joy.

"Oh, my wonderful little bags of weasel guts! I'm so *proud* of you, thinking up that marvellous prank all by yourselves. That's *two* already this morning, and we haven't even finished breakfast! My Mini Mischief-Makers will be Professional Pranksters before I know it!"

Edgar glowed with pride as Elsie continued her cackling. Just then, Mr Odd gave a pained yell and stumbled out of the kitchen, his hands flailing around like an angry windmill. The two baby crocodiles had clamped their tiny jaws on to both of his forefingers.

Mrs Odd and the twins burst out laughing. Tears were streaming down their faces when, all of a sudden, there came a loud CRACK. A second later, Edgar and Elsie found themselves flat on the floor, covered by the contents of the table. Their chairs lay in pieces around them.

"And that's what *we* were doing when *you* went to bed!" cackled Mr Odd, holding up a rusty old saw with one crocodiley hand and pointing a crocodiley finger at them with the other. "Sawing through the legs of your chairs!"

"You did well this morning, kiddly-winkers," said Mrs Odd, patting Edgar and Elsie on their heads. "But you've got to get up pretty early to beat your ma and pa when it comes to prankery!"

"No way!" said Elsie, milk, cereal and soap powder dripping down her snot-green jumper as she got to her feet. "Crocodile eggs beat broken chairs any day of the week!"

"Rubbish!" said Mr Odd. "Look at the mess me and your mother have made! That wins out over little snappers like these." He waggled the crocodiles in the twins' faces.

"You just wait, Dad," said Edgar, wiping porridge off his face. "Elsie and me have been saving up our best pranks for school today."

"I bet it won't beat the pranks I'm gonna pull on those rich folk that've just moved into Snootypants Manor," said Mr Odd.

"Or my pranks on all the folksters rushing to and fro along the high street," said Mrs Odd.

The whole family started arguing and didn't stop for a very long time. Bob groaned to himself and, despite the cold, thought about sleeping outside. He got up and slipped out unnoticed. In all the daily commotion that mealtimes with the Odds brought, no one ever remembered to walk or feed the dog.

Chapter Two

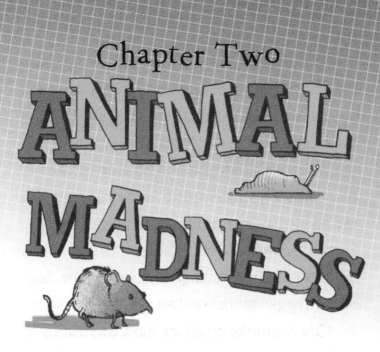

ANIMAL MADNESS

The Odds set off to work from Number 13 Rotten Row with a song in their hearts and pranks on their minds. Meddlers don't have actual jobs like working on a broccoli farm or in a dog shop. Their occupation (unless they're still at school) is full-time Mischief Making. Work, to a Meddler, is as much fun as bouncing on a trampoline whilst eating two chocolate ice creams would be for you or me.

Mr Odd went up the hill to Choffingly Way where all the rich people of Trott lived.

The houses there were big and posh, and all had curtains made of solid gold and toilets that sang to you while you went to the loo. The people of Choffingly Way were so rich they didn't need to work. They just moped around their houses all day, counting their vases and shouting at their servants. Mr Odd could cause an awful lot of mischief in houses like those...

Mrs Odd went down the hill to the high street. The people there were always hustling and bustling backwards and forwards, not watching where they were going with their arms full of shopping. Mrs Odd could cause quite a lot of trouble in a busy place like that...

The Odd twins made their way to St Mumps. Edgar and Elsie didn't do particularly well at school. But, after all, that's not why they went. They went to practise their pranks so that when they left they would be ready to join the family business as Professional Pranksters. And this particular day, Edgar and Elsie knew, would be an extra special day for prankery. Because today was the day they were having a visit from Stan McFlan the Animal Man.

Stan McFlan would drive around to different schools showing bored animals to strange and exotic children. Edgar and Elsie's headmistress, Mrs Missus, had been telling the whole school about the visit for weeks. The fact that everyone would be in the assembly hall at once with live animals was an opportunity too good to miss. Edgar and Elsie had been planning a big prank for some time.

The twins' whole class was buzzing with excitement as they followed their teacher, Mr Surname, into the hall. They chatted about the types of animals they might see and wondered if Stan McFlan would bring any strange and exotic ones, like snakes or lizards or Loch Ness Monsters or dinosaurs.

"I hope he's brought a hippopotamus!" said Sally Vinegar.

"I hope he's got a bald eagle!" said Nathaniel Pink.

"I hope he has a cat!" said Eric Hips, who led quite a sheltered life and had never seen a cat.

Stan McFlan himself was waiting behind the velvet stage curtain, making sure all his animals were ready to show off. Edgar and Elsie traipsed in behind their class. But instead of following them to the back of the hall and sitting down, they slipped behind the stage curtain.

They clambered up the curtain rope and trotted along the curtain rail. Below them, Stan McFlan was pacing back and forth. In his arms was a large green iguana called Martha Jenkins. The rest of his animals sat in their cages underneath a large blanket.

"All right, Edgar," said Elsie. "Phase One of Operation Chaos and Confusion is about to commence."

"Roger that," said Edgar. "Ready?"

"Yup," said Elsie.

"Aren't you going to say '*and don't call me Roger*'?"

"Nope."

From the other side of the curtain, Edgar and Elsie could hear a deathly hush fall as Mrs Missus got up on stage. She was a short woman with violent red hair and a booming voice that could rival a cannon. No one dared cross her. Apart from Edgar and Elsie Odd, that is.

"Good morning, everybody!" boomed Mrs Missus.

"Good morning, Mrs Missus!" the children chimed back in their best collective impression of church bells.

"Well, as I'm sure you know, this morning we're having a visit from Stan McFlan, who's going to show us some of his animals."

"Wait till he steps through the curtain," whispered Elsie to Edgar.

Edgar nodded.

"So," Mrs Missus continued, "without further ado, please welcome Stan McFlan the Animal Man."

Edgar and Elsie held their breath as Stan McFlan hesitated for a second, then stepped through the curtains. Quicker than two jet-powered millipedes, they slid down the curtain ropes and threw off the blanket covering the animals.

Along with Martha the iguana, Stan had brought:

A red and green parrot

A chinchilla

A great big hairy tarantula

A large brown owl

A long, stripy snake

And a goat

"They all look a bit bored, don't they, Elsie?" said Edgar, grinning fiendishly.

"I think they do, Edgar," smirked Elsie. "I know something that might liven them up a bit. Commencing Phase One of Operation Chaos and Confusion."

The twins set to work opening all the creatures' cages. Through the stage curtain they could hear Stan McFlan waffling away.

"Good morning, children," began Stan. "Now, before I show you the animals, I always like to warm up with a little song what I wrote. It goes a little something like this... I'll just count myself in – cockatoo cockathree cockafour:

"I'm Stan McFlan the Animal Man and
I drive around the country in me big, blue van.
I takes all me animals, birds and squids,
And I shows 'em and I tells 'em
to the dear old kids.
Anteaters, rhinos, sharks and mice,
I don't have these, but I do have lice."

There were another twelve-and-a-half verses, but most of them were just naming more animals he didn't have. And other infestations he *did* have. Before long, the children in the hall started to fidget.

"Phase One of Operation Chaos and Confusion complete," said Edgar. "All the cage doors are open. Phase Two can begin..."

"Have you got it?" said Elsie.

Edgar grinned and reached into one of the pockets in his shorts. "Course I have."

Pockets are very important to a Meddler. *The Meddlers' Mischief Manual* states that:

THE MEDDLERS' MISCHIEF MANUAL
CLOTHING: POCKETS

A Meddler should have no fewer than seventeen pockets about his or her person at any one time.

The contents of a Meddler's pockets should, at the very least, contain:

* Live earthworms, slugs or other slimy invertebrates

* Itching powder or the crushed stings of the Black Grunting Scorpions of Darkest Peru Where It's So Dark You Can't Even See Your Own Knees

* Spare pants (elasticated)

* Custard (or similar)

* Eggs (any kind)

* 1 spare Custard Nozzle

* A live shrew called Benjamin.

Keeping many well-stocked pockets allows a working Meddler to rediscover all sorts of helpful items they had forgotten they possessed. To a Meddler there are few things more satisfying than finding a live shrew about their person when nothing else but a live shrew will do.

Edgar brought out a large, bright-red alarm clock with two bright-yellow bells on top. Instead of numbers on the face it had words where the three, six, nine and twelve should've been. They were:

SOON...
NOT YET...
NEARLY...
BOOM!!!

"Ah," Elsie sighed. "Dr Klampit's Patented Al-harm Clock."

"Wakes you up," said Edgar, "and *shakes* you up." He wound it up, then set it down behind the cages. "Phase Two complete."

"On to Phase Three..." grinned Elsie, and she scampered back up the curtain rope, Edgar hot on her heels. They skittered along the curtain pole like crafty rats and slipped out of the hall door just as Stan McFlan started warbling verse nine to an increasingly restless group of children.

"Phase Three..." said Elsie, producing a chain from a skirt pocket and wrapping it round the door handles.

"Complete..." said Edgar, producing a padlock and snapping it shut on the chain.

"On to Phase Four," said Elsie as they came to a crossroads in the corridor. "You know what to do?"

"Please," Edgar smirked. "I could do this with my eyes closed."

They went off in opposite directions. Edgar hurried down to the Year 6 classroom and started stacking the chairs into one huge, teetering pile. Elsie skidded into the Reception Class and did the same. When their arms were full (Meddlers can carry over twelve times their own body weight when it comes to pranking) they ran back out into the corridor.

Edgar made his way down to the Reception Class, crossing paths with Elsie as she ran back up to Year 6. Once they had reached their destinations, they put down the chairs, grabbed some tables and jogged back along the corridor. They did this several more times until, eventually, they had swapped the entire Reception and Year 6 classrooms around. The carpets, the tables, the chairs, the displays, the whiteboards, the book areas, even the storerooms.

But they weren't going to stop at swapping a mere two classrooms. They did their merry little dance all over again – and AGAIN – until they'd switched every classroom in St Mumps.

Year 5 became Year 1, Year 1 became Year 5.

Year 4 became Year 2, Year 2 became Year 4.

Year 3, however, was a different story. They had run out of classrooms to swap it with. So, in a stroke of brilliance, they simply moved all the chairs, tables, the whiteboard and displays around so the room was facing the opposite way.

"Phase Four complete," said Edgar breathlessly.

"Phase Five begins..." wheezed Elsie, looking at her watch. "Any second now! Come on!"

Back in the hall, Stan McFlan was finally about to finish his overly long song and reveal his collection of very bored animals. The twins peeped through the window just in time to see the curtains open on the animals. The children of St Mumps all started craning their necks to try and get a better look.

"Wait for it..." Elsie was counting the seconds.

"Oh my!" said Stan McFlan. "It looks like all the cages are open!"

"Any second..." said Edgar, who was dancing on the spot with excitement.

"I'll soon sort this out," said Stan McFlan,

rolling up his sleeves. "Luckily, my animals are very well trained... Can anyone hear an alarm clock?"

"NOW!" Edgar and Elsie screamed together, as a tremendous RRRRRRIIIINNNGGGG! echoed around St Mumps, shaking the school from its rafters to its foundations.

The children screamed.

Stan McFlan yelped.

The animals screeched, squawked, hooted, hissed, bleated and made terrified tarantula noises as they leaped from their cages and out among the assembled children of St Mumps.

Operation Chaos and Confusion was aptly named. The next few minutes were a blur of shrieks and yells, and parrot and owl poo. Everyone rushed to the doors to get out, but the way was barred by a very angry-looking goat who threatened to butt anyone that came near. In all it took a total of four teachers, a caretaker and eight dinnerladies armed with ladles to chase the angry goat away from the doors, only to find they were locked.

Stan McFlan was running around like a headless guinea pig. "COME BACK, ME BEAUTIES, COME TO DADDYKINS!" he cried, trying to get his beasties back in their cages. The next thing anyone knew, he was being chased around the hall by an angry goat.

"Wait for it..." said Edgar, grinning at the ensuing chaos. "Any minute now..."

"THE FIRE EXIT!" shouted a helpful art teacher by the name of Mr Philpotts. "EVERYBODY OUT THROUGH THE FIRE EXIT!"

"There it is," sighed Elsie. "Perfection."

Before anyone could stop him, Mr Philpotts had barged the fire exit wide open. Which would have been fine. If it hadn't been connected to the automatic sprinkler system.

The already ear-splitting shrieks grew louder as the panicky people inside the hall became very *wet* and panicky people.

"EVERYBODY OUT!" gargled Mr Philpotts, as his mouth filled up with water.

The pupils and teachers of St Mumps made a mad dash for the fire exit, pushing and shoving their way out into the playground. Edgar and Elsie snuck outside and joined their class, unnoticed in the chaos.

A very soggy Animal Man began collecting up his very soggy animals, starting with a big and hairy tarantula that had taken shelter in a Year 3 boy's hair.

"Right, everybody!" bellowed Mrs Missus. "I think that's enough excitement for one day. Back to your classrooms!"

Edgar and Elsie grinned.

"The Final Phase begins..." said Edgar.

Chapter Three

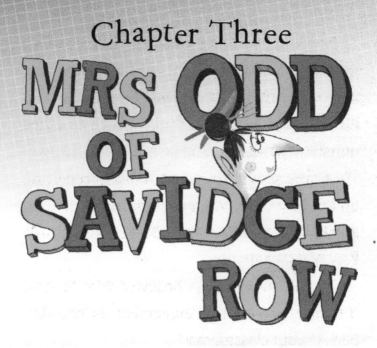

MRS ODD OF SAVIDGE ROW

Meanwhile, in the high street Mrs Odd was having quite a busy day herself. She had already tripped up three pedestrians – one carrying a huge cake, one holding too many bags of shopping and the other walking eight large, slobbery dogs.

Hiding behind a lamp post, Mrs Odd peeped out as a businessman approached, swinging his briefcase to and fro and checking his watch. He was wearing a smart suit, an even smarter bowtie and an *even smarter* bowler hat.

Slipping out from her hiding place, Mrs Odd leaped stealthily on to the swinging briefcase without the man even noticing. She swung back and forth like a pendulum as the man marched down the street, barging people out of the way. With two clicks Mrs Odd undid the silver clasps on his briefcase, and a shower of papers and documents cascaded into the air, littering the road and pavement.

"What the— Oh no!" cried the man, rushing to pick them up.

At that moment, a gust of wind blew the papers in every direction. The man dived into the road, grabbing, leaping and grasping for all he was worth. Some people started grabbing, leaping and grasping too; others stopped and laughed. Drivers slammed on their brakes and shouted rude words out of their windows. Words like:

Mrs Odd watched from a striped awning above a shop – a most excellent viewing platform for a Meddler to observe her pranks. It was then that she noticed where she was. Savidge Row, a string of shops where all the rich money-baggers came to have their hair dyed gold and their poodles dry-cleaned. The awning she was sitting on belonged to:

**TAYLOR & TAYLOR & SONS & SONS –
QUALITY CLOTHING**

Mrs Odd smiled to herself as potential pranking opportunities flooded her menacing little mind. Whipping the knife and fork from her hair, she swiftly undid the lock on the upstairs window and snuck inside. She found herself in a large store room. There were several tailor's dummies, a few crates of pins, buttons and scraps of material, and row after row of smart suits and dresses, all hung up and waiting to be collected.

Downstairs the bell rang as a customer entered the shop. A few moments later, Mrs Odd heard someone marching up the stairs. Hiding behind a dummy, she peeked out and saw a large, portly man. It was one of the Taylors.

Mr Taylor marched over to the rows of suits and picked out a dreary beige one, turned to the door and shouted down, "Is it the medium beige with the frilly lapels and trousers with the altered hems, Mrs Monk-Statham? I'm all on my own today, you see, and I can't be marching up and down these stairs any more than I have to. Not with my back the way it is, you understand."

"That's right, Mr Taylor!" Mrs Monk-Statham called, and Mr Taylor went downstairs with the suit. Then Mrs Odd heard the bell on the door ring as Mrs Monk-Statham left the shop.

By now, Mrs Odd's devious little brain-box had thought up the beginnings of a very fine prank.

She skulked over to the crate of pins. (Meddlers *never* walk, they always skulk or creep.)

With one big shove, Mrs Odd heaved the whole crate over. It landed with an almighty CRASH!, spilling tiny pins all over the floor. Then, moving quickly, she pushed over the crate of buttons and the crate full of scraps of material. Both landed with satisfying THUDS. From downstairs she heard Mr Taylor cry, "What in heaven's name was that?"

As Mr Taylor came marching up the stairs once more, Mrs Odd hid behind the door.

"How on *earth*...?" Mr Taylor stamped one of his large feet. "This is the very limit! I shall have to shut the shop and sort this mess out at once. I can't very well have sharp little pins mixed in with my buttons and scraps of spare material. Why, I might accidentally stab someone when I'm doing an alteration."

He stomped back downstairs, turned the OPEN sign to CLOSED and marched back up again, carrying a large cup of coffee. He placed it on a box of tape measures and got to work sorting out the pins from the buttons and scraps.

Mrs Odd grabbed a small scrap for her own mischief-makings, snuck out of the storeroom and quietly shut the door behind her.

Tippy-toeing downstairs, she skulked across the shop floor and wrapped the piece of scrap material round the clapper in the bell above the front door. Then she turned the CLOSED sign to OPEN and waited for the next customer.

While she was waiting, she found a box full of customers' phone numbers and addresses, which were all filed neatly in alphabetical order on little cards. "Hmm..." Mrs Odd hmmed to herself. "My superior Meddling brain tells me that the people on these cards are to be contacted when their clothes are ready to be picked up. Well, I think it's time I made a few *adjustments* to Mr and Mr Taylor's system..."

She resisted the urge simply to put them all in the wrong order (that would be rather amateurish for a Professional Prankster) and instead went about changing the phone numbers on every single card. Where there was a number 1 she changed it to a number 7, where there was a 3, she turned it into an 8 and so on. This was tremendous fun for Mrs Odd, as it was the sort of prank that would stretch over a long period of time. *The Meddlers' Mischief Manual* calls this type of prank The Long Prank.

THE MEDDLERS' MISCHIEF MANUAL
THE LONG PRANK

The Long Prank is any prank that will aggravate or annoy a prankee (or victim) over a long period of time. Good examples of this prank are:

* Altering addresses/names/phone numbers in address books
* Swapping one cupboard's contents with another's
* Constant condiment swapping (sugar for salt, ketchup for washing-up liquid, etc.)

There are many others out there waiting to be discovered. Be creative.

Just then, the door opened and in walked a very flustered-looking gentleman. He wore a smart suit, an even smarter bowtie and an *even smarter* bowler hat. Clasped awkwardly in his arms were piles of papers and it was with a little squeak of excitement that Mrs Odd recognized the businessman she had pranked only a few minutes earlier.

"Can I help you, sir?" asked Mrs Odd in her finest lady shop-owner's voice.

"No, you cannot!" snapped the businessman. "Not unless you can turn back the clock so I can get to my meeting on time, or else stop my briefcase from bursting open in the middle of the street, making my very important and complicated businessman-like papers go flying all over the place! Or even better, if you could explain why someone called me dunder-chump earlier!"

Mrs Odd tried very hard to suppress her giggles. "I'm sorry, sir," she said, "I can't do anything like that. I've no idea what dunder-chump means. Or speckle-chops for that matter. Are you here to pick up a suit?"

"Well, of *course* I am!" the businessman snapped once again. "Why else would I be here? To eat a barbecued rhinoceros?"

"And your surname is...?" Mrs Odd was starting to think she hadn't pranked this very rude man half as badly as he deserved.

"My *name*?" he shrieked. "Why, I've been coming to this establishment for years; surely you should know *me*?"

"I'm new," Mrs Odd replied in her finest I'm-new voice.

"It's Urmston. Mr Charles Urmston," said Mr Charles Urmston.

"I'll be right back with your suit, Mr Urmston, Mr Charles Urmston." Mrs Odd bowed low and backed out of the room, creeping up the stairs without making a sound.

Upstairs in the storeroom, Mr Taylor was too engrossed in his sorting to notice Mrs Odd open the door and slink over to the rows of clothes.

She quietly flicked through them. But far from checking the name on each ticket, she was instead searching for a new outfit for Mr Urmston. Finding just what she needed, she silently removed it from the rail and grabbed Mr Taylor's cup of coffee from the crate of tape measures.

When Mrs Odd returned, Mr Urmston was trying to arrange his papers into some sort of order. His briefcase was open on the counter and beside it lay his bowler hat. He seemed to be getting angrier with each bit of paper he picked up, and soon looked as though his head might well explode.

Mrs Odd approached. "Here we are, Mr Urmston, Mr Charles Urmston – your suit. *And* I've brought you a nice cup of coffee."

Mr Urmston did not look up from his papers. "I don't like coffee," he barked, holding out his hand. Still not looking up, he barked, "Suit!"

But rather than handing him the suit, Mrs Odd handed him the cup of lukewarm coffee.

Mr Urmston, expecting a heavy suit on a hanger, made to swing the suit over his shoulder, but instead swung the cup of coffee over his head.

The contents oozed down him, from his neatly slicked hair to his new suede shoes, covering his suit and shirt in sticky brown liquid. He stopped stock still. "Why you ... idiotic ... doddering ... speckle-chopped..."

"Oh, I'm sorry, Mr Urmston," said Mrs Odd, clasping her hands together in mock horror. "I thought you said *coffee* when you held out your hand."

"I said *suit*, you mad menace, SUIT! It doesn't sound anything *like* COFFEE! Now look at me! What am I going to do? I've got to be in a very important meeting in..." he glanced at his watch, which had just at that moment stopped working as coffee seeped its way inside, "...twelve minutes ago!"

"Well, not to worry," said Mrs Odd. "I've just had an idea! Why don't you wear your new suit to your meeting?" Before Mr Urmston could reply, Mrs Odd had whipped off his jacket, shirt and trousers, leaving him standing there in nothing but his vest, pinstriped underpants and socks.

"Now then..." Mrs Odd unwrapped Mr Urmston's new outfit and, quick as a flash, threw it on over his head. It was a large and very frilly tartan dress. Mrs Odd was faster than a frog out of a frying pan as she stuffed Mr Urmston's bowler hat on to his head and bundled his coffee-stained suit, briefcase and mass of papers into his arms.

"Off you go then, Mr Urmston!" She wheeled him out of the shop before he could say a word. "If you run all the way and don't stop, you might just make your meeting!"

Mr Urmston stumbled out of the shop and into the high street, his hands too full of his briefcase, papers and coffee-stained clothing to notice that he now looked like a mad, bowler-hat-wearing Scottish lady.

Mrs Odd watched from the window, chuckling. "What a dunder-chump!"

Chapter Four

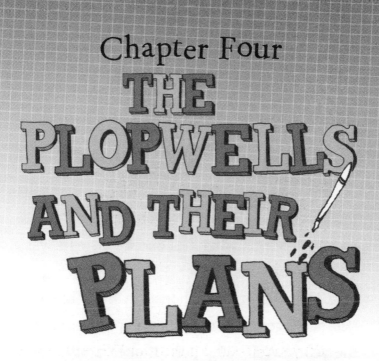

THE PLOPWELLS AND THEIR PLANS

Up on Choffingly Way, Mr Odd had also been having rather a productive morning. After picking a new wilted dandelion for his buttonhole, he had sloped into five different houses, causing more and more mischief as he went along. (Sloping is a bit like skulking, only slopier.)

It's good for a Meddler to work up to their biggest prank of the day – it gives them something to aim for. Mr Odd's favourite prank so far was letting Mrs Wimbledon-Flumpstanton's poodle, Flopsy-Wopsy, loose in her make-up drawer. Flopsy-Wopsy looked like a yapping stick of candyfloss by the time she had finished eating Mrs Wimbledon-Flumpstanton's lipstick and rolling around in her rouge.

Mr Odd was still chuckling to himself, remembering Mrs Wimbledon-Flumpstanton's shrieks of horror, when he noticed where he was.

"Snootypants Manor..." he said, gazing in awe at the grand old house in front of him. "Home to generations of Snootypantses down the years. Well, why don't I takes a little look inside and see who it is that's moved in."

Sneaking up to the door, Mr Odd hid in a hanging basket, keeping an eye out for servants. When he was sure the coast was clear, he nipped through the letterbox, but not before making certain his shoes were caked in soil. Stomping merrily down the newly carpeted hallway, Mr Odd resisted the urge to spell out rude words with his muddy footprints and made his way into the kitchen. There was, after all, a lot of mischief to make and not a lot of time to make it in.

The kitchen was a brand-new, never-been-used-before-and-too-nice-to-use-for-actually-cooking-in, sparkly type of kitchen. "Oh, if only Mrs Odd was here to see this," he sighed. Mrs Odd liked nothing more than a nice clean and sparkly kitchen that she could mess up.

Mr Odd went over to the fridge to see if it was well-stocked with eggs and ketchup.

THE MEDDLERS' MISCHIEF MANUAL
HOMES: KITCHENS

Kitchens are a Professional Prankster's fail-safe favourite for fun and frolics! A few eggs balanced to fall as soon as the fridge is opened or a squeezy ketchup bottle carefully placed where someone might tread on it are pranking classics. The best sort of Professional Prankster makes their victim think it was all their fault for not stacking the eggs properly or putting the ketchup away.

He was just about to open the fridge door when something shiny caught his eye. On the kitchen table was a bunch of keys. Shiny things have the same effect on a Meddler as on a magpie. They are mesmerized by them. Especially keys. Meddlers love keys.

So pretty...

So shiny...

So easy to hide.

One of the earliest pranks on modern man was hiding keys. Of course, Meddlers had to wait until locks were invented, but a few minutes after, keys started going missing. As a popular twist on the prank, they would sometimes replace them with identical keys that opened absolutely nothing.

Mr Odd drifted over to the table in a daze and stared at the bunch of keys that lay there, all shiny and key-like. He reached into his pocket and brought out a bunch of fake keys to fashion an identical but useless set. Just as he plucked the keys from the table, he noticed something beneath them. It was a large blue sheet of paper. Bold white letters at the top read:

THE PLOPWELL PLAZA MEGA-SUPERMARKET

Mr Odd recognized at once that these were the blueprints for a building, and rubbed his hands together with glee.

He leaped up to the table to take a closer look. He had already begun putting seesaws in the car park and at least four huge escalators that led straight into brick walls when he heard the front door open.

Mr Odd leaped away from the table as quick as a greasy cobra and shut himself in the cutlery drawer. From inside he could hear two people talking excitedly as they entered the kitchen. He opened the drawer just a tiny bit and popped one pointy ear out so he could listen.

"Well, Mrs Plopwell," came a posh man's voice, "that meeting with Mr Urmston went exceedingly well, if I do say so myself. I think he's very close to putting forward our proposal."

"Indeed it did, Mr Plopwell," came a posh woman's voice. "I think one more visit and a nice little *donation* from our piggy bank might just do the trick. Though why did Mr Urmston turn up dressed like your mad Scottish Auntie Linda?"

"I'm not sure," Mr Plopwell replied. "Startling resemblance, though. He kept muttering something about a strange lady at the tailor's..."

Mr Odd beamed with pride. Mrs Odd was working the high street today, and dressing men up like mad aunties sounded like her sort of prank. "Well done, my little lobster," he muttered.

"Well, whatever his reason, it worked," said Mrs Plopwell. "Mr Urmston seemed very impressed with all our ideas."

"And we're sure to win over the mayor with the huge sack of cash we'll offer him to seal the deal," said the man, and they both cackled like insane herons.

Something about that cackle made Mr Odd's nose hairs tremble. He was certain he had heard it somewhere before. He risked poking one eye out of the drawer to get a good look at the pair. Luckily, they were so busy guffawing at their own joke that they didn't see Mr Odd's beady little eye peering out at them.

The man had a bushy moustache. He wore a tweed suit, a floppy cap, a white scarf round his neck and flying goggles perched on his head. His lady wife wore spiky high heels. She had long rolls of curly hair the colour of ripe bananas, upon which sat a diamond tiara. She was draped in a huge coat that looked like it was made from the fur of poor tiny baby orphan squirrels.

"Did you see all those filthy, horrid pigeons we passed on the way home?" said Mrs Plopwell, her face turning so wrinkly in disgust it resembled a constipated prune.

"They weren't pigeons, dear," said Mr Plopwell, "they were children."

"Oh yes," said Mrs Plopwell. "Either way, nasty little disease-riddled snot-jockeys."

"I quite agree," Mr Plopwell agreed. "Verminous gas-filled trump-monkeys. It was all I could do not to run them over with dear old *Ploppy 1.*"

"But that car is your prized possession, darling!" said Mrs Plopwell. "You wouldn't want to go getting children splattered all over it, would you?"

Mr Plopwell shuddered. "All this talk of children is making me feel sick to my tummy."

"I know what'll make you feel better," said Mrs Plopwell. "Let's build a huge swimming pool."

"But we already have one of those in the conservatory," said Mr Plopwell.

"Yes," said Mrs Plopwell, "but this one can be smack dab in the middle of the front garden so all the neighbourhood children can see it. We'll install a wave machine, waterslides, fountains and then ... NOT let any children come and play in it!"

Mr Plopwell laughed. "What an excellent idea, darling," he said, wiping a rich tear from his left eye. "And while we're at it, let's put in an underwater toyshop and sweetshop."

The Plopwells both cackled another high-pitched, insane cackle. Mr Odd had to cover his ears it was so awful. Where *had* he heard it before?

"Those nasty, needle-nosed nit-nashers," said Mr Odd to himself. "I'll teach those rich hobgobblers a lesson."

While both of their backs were turned, Mr Odd stole out of the drawer, pocketing a few silver teaspoons as he went, and crept up behind them. Reaching into Mr Plopwell's pocket, he quietly lifted out a large set of fancy car keys for a large, fancy car. Looking down, he saw the kitchen floor was made up of shiny marble tiles. Lifting one up with a bony hand, he slipped the keys underneath and let the tile drop with a small THUD.

At this noise (small as it was) the Plopwells turned round. Now you might think it strange, not to mention extremely unprofessional, that a Professional Prankster of Mr Odd's ability would make a noise whilst up to no good. Well, you'll be pleased to know that it was all part of Mr Odd's cunning plan...

By the time the Plopwells turned round to see what the noise was, Mr Odd was already swinging from the chandelier by his muddy-shoed feet.

"What was that noise?" said Mr Plopwell.

"I don't know," replied Mrs Plopwell. "It sounded like a tile being lifted up and dropped again so as to cause a distraction, thus making us turn round."

"Indeed," said Mr Plopwell, impressed as ever

by his wife's incredible knack for working out the possible reasons for mysterious sounds. "No matter, we're far too rich and carefree to care about strange little sounds we hear in our kitchen. What say we go for a drive and celebrate, eh?"

"What a lovely idea," said Mrs Plopwell. "But what are we celebrating?"

"Why, the fact we're about to get the go ahead to build our fancy new Mega-Supermarket, of course!"

"Of course!" Mrs Plopwell replied. "Have you got your keys?"

Mr Odd sniggered as Mr Plopwell searched every pocket. "I'm sure I had them in here somewhere..." he muttered, as he patted himself all over like he was a really good dog. Mr Odd was waiting for Mr Plopwell to start turning his fancy new house upside down in search of his keys, when something strange happened.

"Oh well," cried Mr Plopwell, throwing his rich hands into the air. "I can't find the ruddy things. Never mind, I'll just use a spare set."

Mr Odd suddenly felt a tingling in the tips of his fingers and toes. The ends of his ears and nose went numb and his eyebrows twitched.

Mr Plopwell went over to a cupboard and opened it. Inside were hundreds of spare keys. Far too many for even a prankster of Mr Odd's delicate skill to whisk away without dropping any. Mr Plopwell then plucked a set from a hook and jangled them at his wife. "Ready to go?"

"Ready!"

"Oh," said Mr Plopwell, "and while we're out, we can drop off the final building plans at Mr Urmston's office so he can have a look at them before our meeting with the mayor."

"Capital idea!" said Mrs Plopwell. "Tally-ho!"

And off they went, scooping the plans up off the table before skipping out of the door. Mr Odd skulked after them, feeling rather a failure.

Once outside, the Plopwells got into their fancy open-top car as Mr Odd slipped inside a large dustbin. The car's number plate read *Ploppy 1* and, almost as if they knew Mr Odd was listening and wanted to add insult to injury, Mr Plopwell said, "This is *such* an amazing car. I can't believe anyone would be so stupid as to think I'd only have the one set of keys. This little beauty is my pride and joy." He stroked the dashboard lovingly before turning on the engine.

The engine roared into life like a noisy lion, making Mr Odd jump and bang his head on the dustbin lid.

Just before the car roared away, Mrs Plopwell waved the blueprints at Mr Plopwell and said, "Remind me, darling, what's the name of that dreadful little street we're bulldozing to make way for our Mega-Supermarket?"

Mr Plopwell grinned as he pulled down his flying goggles. "I think it's called Rotten Row, dear. Yes, that's it, Rotten Row. Dirty, horrid little street it is. I dare say Trott will be a finer place without it. Tally-ho!"

And they zoomed off down the hill, leaving a shocked and sore-headed Mr Odd staring after them, wearing a dustbin lid for a hat.

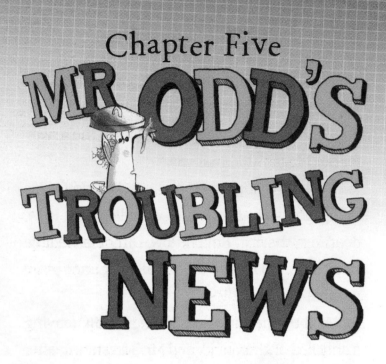

Chapter Five
MR ODD'S TROUBLING NEWS

Mr Odd was late home that evening. He slumped through the door of Number 13, still wearing the dustbin lid on his head.

Bob lollopped over to greet him, his flea-bitten tail wagging, his head raised ready for a scratch from his master's filthy fingernails. But Mr Odd walked straight past him.

He flumped down in his favourite patchy old armchair in such a daze, he barely even noticed the giant mousetrap the twins had put on the seat as it pinched his bony bottom.

"What's the matter, Dad?" asked Edgar, stopping in mid-guffaw at his father's expressionless face. "You usually love the giant-mousetrap-on-the-chair prank."

"But that's *nothing* compared with the prank we pulled today at school, Dad!" said Elsie.

The twins spent the next few minutes telling Mr Odd about Operation Chaos and Confusion in between fits of giggles.

By the time they had finished, Edgar could hardly breathe for laughing. "The infants started learning long division while the Year 6 kids made plasticine dinosaurs!"

"It took them till lunchtime to figure it out, then everyone spent the rest of the day changing everything back," said Elsie, rolling around on the floor.

"They didn't even get halfway through before the hometime bell rang!" Edgar was doubled up, clutching his stomach. "So Mrs Missus said all the teachers had to stay behind."

"Ah, they've done us proud today," said Mrs Odd. She glanced up from the socks she was darning by the fire (sewing up the holes you put your feet in) and turned to her husband. "Is everything all right, my little cat-steamer? You seem a bit pink around the gills. The colour's all rushing back to your normally pale and lifeless-looking skin. What's wrong?"

Mr Odd looked up at his family. Oh, what a wonderful, sneaky, reeky, give-you-lots-of-cheeky family he had. And his home. His fabulous smelly, nelly, you'd-never-be-able-to-selly home, complete with its damp patches, mould, curtain-lice and carpet-nits. And, of course, his dear old dog, Bob.

"Family," said Mr Odd, taking the dustbin lid off his head and dropping it to the floor with a CLANG. "I have some terrible, frightening and altogether quite scarifying news."

"What is it?" asked Elsie.

"Well, I was up at Snootypants Manor today, looking to prank them new penny-jinglers that've just moved in. I tried to prank 'em by hiding their keys, but ... they had a spare set. Loads of spare sets, actually. Too many keys for even me to hide."

"But you've hidden loads of things before," said Edgar.

"Like all those fish fingers from that fish-finger van," said Elsie.

"Or that truckload of tree toads," said Mrs Odd.

"Don't forget all those glow-in-the-dark pipe-cleaners," added Edgar. "And that was at night!"

"I know, I know," said Mr Odd. "But this was different... This time I got ... *The Shudders*!"

The Odds gasped.

"The Shudders, my little eel?" said Mrs Odd, clasping a hand over her mouth. "Are you sure?"

"As sure as taters aren't turnips," said Mr Odd. "I got that terrible feeling that all Meddlers get when a prank is about to go wrong. I can't remember the last time I felt it. But I know what it was, and it was The Shudders."

THE MEDDLERS' MISCHIEF MANUAL
THE SHUDDERS

The Shudders is an ancient Meddling warning signal that all Meddlers possess. A Meddler will get The Shudders when a prank is about to go wrong, backfire, or go unnoticed. They may feel a number of different sensations, but the most common are:

* A tingling in the fingers and toes
* A numbing in the tips of the ears and nose
* Minor eyebrow twitching
* Nose hair plaiting

When experiencing The Shudders, one must remain calm. A Professional Prankster should gather his or her wits and try again almost immediately. However, there is no shame in admitting defeat and trying again another day. Do not be discouraged!

Mrs Odd, Edgar and Elsie all went quiet.

"But that's not the worst of it, my troop of howler monkeys," said Mr Odd. He took a deep breath. "They said they were going to bulldoze Rotten Row to make way for something called a *Mega-Supermarket*."

"But they can't!" said Edgar. "I love this house. It's centrally located, which makes it ideal for pranking."

Everyone looked at him.

"Well, it *is*! And where else am I going to find so many dead earwigs for my Dead Earwig Collection?" He pulled out his Matchbox of Dead Earwigs that he carried everywhere with him and looked at it lovingly.

Mrs Odd put her hands on her hips. "We'll just have to stop them then, won't we?"

"Yeah!" agreed the twins, both adopting their best *We'll-just-have-to-stop-them-then,-won't-we* faces.

"I don't know," said Mr Odd, getting up from his armchair and removing the giant mousetrap from his bony bottom. "There was somethin' about them two..."

"What do you mean?" asked Mrs Odd, frowning.

"I mean," said Mr Odd, who couldn't remember the last time a prank of his had gone wrong, "I tried pranking them there and then, but it was like they was one step ahead of me. Almost like they was *aware*..."

The entire Odd family shivered. For a Meddler, being spotted or having a victim become aware of your presence is their worst nightmare. Worse than that one where you have to sing "Happy Birthday" in front of the entire school and you forget the words. *And* your clothes. It's best summed up in *The Meddlers' Mischief Manual* under the heading BEING SPOTTED.

THE MEDDLERS' MISCHIEF MANUAL
BEING SPOTTED

DON'T BE!!!

HOWEVER...

A Meddler may present him/herself to a victim if:
* The victim is too flustered to notice you properly
* The Meddler is in disguise
* The victim is a complete jam-magnet

"And that laugh," said Mr Odd, his eyes glazing over as he remembered. "That 'orrible, 'orrible laugh... I'm sure I've heard it somewhere before..."

He went silent again and started to pace the room.

Mrs Odd tried her best to shake off the terrible feeling she got whenever she thought of one of her family being seen whilst prankifying. "You know, we *could* always find another place to live," she suggested. "Maybe even move to another town. Or to the city?"

Mr Odd stopped his pacing. "The city? Oh no, my little dingo-breath, we've got a sweet deal living in Trott. Do you know how many Meddlers are lining up to get positions here? Why, every time I see the Weirdlys or the Creeps, they're always telling me how much pranking there is to be done in the city, and how it's such a great place to raise kids, and how we should do a house-swap some time. But I know their game, the little tricklers. They'll take our house and never give it back!

It's the same with the Nobodys. They've all got designs on our house *and* on Trott. I knows they 'ave! No, we don't belong in the cities, not with all them CITV cameras they've got everywhere these days. I'm telling yer, it's getting harder and harder for a Meddler to meddle in this day and age."

"They're called See-See-TV cameras, Dad," said Edgar, rolling his eyes at Elsie.

"Yeah, Dad," said Elsie. "Because they see everything you do. Twice."

Mr Odd huffed. "Well, whatever they're called, we ain't being scared out of town by no measly money-mongers and that's final."

"We can't move, we love St Mumps!" said Edgar. "The kids and teachers are so easy to prank!"

"And besides," added Elsie, "at any other school they might actually try to *teach* us things. We'd have far less time for pranks if that was the case!"

"The children are right," said Mr Odd. "This is our home and this is where we belong."

"But what are we going to do?" asked Mrs Odd.

Mr Odd thought for a moment. "I'm taking each of you off your individual pranking duties. Mrs Odd, from now on you can leave the accidents you cause so well to happen ... *by accident*. And twins?" He looked down at Edgar and Elsie. "I'm taking you two out of school. It's not like you'll miss anything. In fact, this'll probably be a lot more educational than learning that Canberra is the capital of Australia."

"No, that's Wazzamondaloolachimp," said Edgar and Elsie together. Geography was not their best subject.

"I'll tell you what we're going to do," said Mr Odd, who was now standing as though there was triumphant music playing somewhere nearby. "We're going to stop pranking one another and join forces! Together, with our combined talents, we're going to chase those rich little snootle-mumpits right out of Trott! Are you with me?"

"Absolutely! But wait there a minute..." said Mrs Odd, scurrying out of the room, "I've just got to take the giant-and-easily-startled scorpions out from under the twins' pillows."

At that, Edgar and Elsie made to scuttle off too.

"And where are you going?" asked Mr Odd, a little disappointed that his speech hadn't got a round of applause. Or at least a "woo" from a passing owl.

"To take the rattlesnakes out from under *your* pillows," the twins replied.

Chapter Six
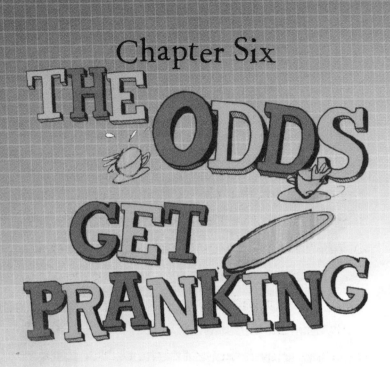
THE ODDS GET PRANKING

Meddlers aren't really designed to work together. It's not in their nature. Sometimes it works, as with Edgar and Elsie, but any more than two Meddlers working together can lead to problems. In fact, in most cases it's almost impossible for just two Meddlers to behave for more than a few seconds before one tries to glue the other's hands inside their pockets and put toads up their trouser legs and then sew them up. So it took the Odds quite a while to make a start on their plans to stop the Plopwells from turning Rotten Row into a vast supermarket. The Plopwell Pranking Plans, they called them.

Long into the night, the Odds sat and planned. In fact, the name of the plan was all they came up with. They did, however, manage to play an awful lot of pranks on each other, most of which involved toads, trouser legs and a needle and thread. So with naught but a name for a plan, the Odds gathered in the Plopwells' kitchen early the next morning.

Peering over the side of the chandelier, the Odds observed the Plopwells' butler, a man by the name of Stipplewick, preparing their breakfast. He was loading two trays with plates of boiled eggs and caviar on toast, and copies of *The Rich People Times*.

"Right, you lot!" Mr Odd addressed his troops as they swung gently back and forth. "We've got ter get these rich twits out of our town. Now I know we didn't exactly come up with a plan... But a good Meddler can think on his or her feet, so let's see what we can come up with off the cuff. We need to prank the Plopwells good and proper. Make 'em hate Trott so they can't wait to get out of here and build their stupid Mega-Supermarket somewhere else. Any ideas?"

"I'll see what I can do," said Edgar, rummaging around in his pockets.

"I'm sure we'll think of something," said Elsie, doing the same.

When no one was looking, the twins leaped from the chandelier and scampered up to the breakfast trays. With one fast, well-rehearsed motion, they swapped the two soft-boiled eggs with eggs from their pranking pockets. Quick as a flash, they hurled themselves back up on to the chandelier.

"What's in those eggs?" asked Mrs Odd.

"We picked them up when we got the crocodile eggs we pranked you with the other day," giggled Elsie.

"Yeah, we're not sure what's in them," sniggered Edgar. "Could be anything. Baby pterodactyls, hedgehogs, mice, hippos..."

"Good work," Mr Odd grinned. "Let's follow him and take a look."

The Odds scuttled upstairs to the Plopwells' bedroom, always keeping a few steps behind Stipplewick and making less noise than a clam in carpet slippers. Finally, Stipplewick stopped outside a great golden door and, balancing the trays, knocked smartly three times.

"Enter!" came Mr Plopwell's voice from inside.

Stipplewick opened the door and set the trays down on a large table inlaid with mirrors. Mrs Plopwell liked to look at her face from as many different angles as possible.

"Your breakfasts, sir and madam," said Stipplewick, bowing so low his eyelashes tickled the carpet.

"Well, it's about time!" snapped Mrs Plopwell from the bed. "I've been awake..." She checked her fancy rich-person's watch. "...Four minutes and nineteen seconds!"

"My apologies, madam," said Stipplewick. "May I proceed to feeding you now?"

"Yes," snapped Mr Plopwell, "and get a move on, I'm starving!"

The Odds watched in amazement from their hiding place on a bookshelf as Stipplewick proceeded to slice up the Plopwells' caviar on toast, spear it on to a fork and then reach over to the bed and place the food into their mouths. Next, Stipplewick picked up a small silver spoon in each hand and, with a deft swipe like a breakfast ninja, he lopped off the top of each egg. The shells landed on the trays and spun like breakdancers as Stipplewick dug the spoons into the eggs. The Plopwells' mouths were open like baby birds awaiting regurgitated worms from their mother.

But instead of digging out spoonfuls of lovely, runny egg, Stipplewick dug out two huge lizards. The lizards sat on the spoons, flicking their lizardy tongues at the Plopwells. The Odds, peering out from behind volumes 5, 6, 7 and 8 of *How to be Rude to Your Servants*, clamped their hands over each other's mouths as they waited for the shrieking to begin.

But Mrs Plopwell merely glanced at the lizards and said, "That egg looks a bit funny. I think it's underdone. Though never having done any cooking before, I can't be sure."

"Hmmm..." said Mr Plopwell. "I think these are a pair of Spiny Nicaraguan Spitting Lizards, dear. Stipplewick must have picked up the wrong eggs this morning. Stipplewick, put them in the terrarium with the rest and then load yourself into the Servant-Be-Gone catapult, would you?"

"Very good, sir," said Stipplewick, walking over to a wardrobe door and opening it. Inside, instead of clothes and pants and things, there was a huge glass tank containing various lizards, four disgruntled tortoises, several rare snakes (including two exotic Feather Boas), eight species of tree frog and a man-eating terrapin.

Glancing into the wardrobe, Mr Odd also spotted a cage containing a strange, stripy bird. "Look!" he pointed. "Do you see it?"

"What?" asked Mrs Odd.

"In that cage," said Mr Odd. "It looks like a—" But before he could finish, Stipplewick had placed the Spiny Nicaraguan Spitting Lizards in the tank and closed the wardrobe door.

"What was it, Dad?" asked Elsie.

"I'm not sure..." said Mr Odd. "I thought it was a... No, I must've got it wrong. What is *he* doing?"

Stipplewick had proceeded to climb inside a large, circular bowl that was attached to a long, bent piece of wood. "Shall I do the honours, sir? Madam?" he asked politely.

"If you would, Stipplewick," said Mr Plopwell.

"Goodbye, sir, madam," said Stipplewick, and he pulled back a large lever. With a mighty TWANG, the Servant-Be-Gone catapult shot him across the room and out of the open window.

"You really *can't* get the staff these days, can you?" said Mrs Plopwell, getting out of bed with a sigh. She walked over to another wardrobe and opened it. A slightly shorter butler named Stumpworth stepped out. As he did so, the Plopwells' twenty-nine remaining spare butlers, all standing neatly one in front of the other, each took a step forward. Mrs Plopwell then closed the door.

"Shall I fetch you something else, sir? Madam?" said Stumpworth.

"No," said Mr Plopwell, who had never said please or thank you in his life. "Just dress us. With your eyes closed, of course. I don't want you gawping at my rich, naked body."

"Of course not, sir," said Stumpworth.

The Odds flitted out of the bedroom door as fast as they could. They didn't want to see Mr Plopwell's rich, naked body, either.

"Well," said Mr Odd, scratching his stubbly chin. "It was a good try, Edgar and Elsie, but I think we need to give something else a go."

"I don't understand," said Edgar. "Mum got really freaked out when we switched her eggs with those crocodile eggs."

"We're obviously dealing with a different teapot of tadpoles here," said Mrs Odd, quoting a famous Meddler saying. Others can be found in *The Meddlers' Mischief Manual*.

THE MEDDLERS' MISCHIEF MANUAL
ANCIENT MEDDLING SAYINGS
AND PROVERBS

* Seven days without a prank makes one weak
* Never disturb a Meddler when they're in the Pranking Zone
* Look after your pranking hands and they'll look after you
* Never nick from other nickers
* Don't whack yourself over the head with a mallet cos it'll hurt

"But," Mrs Odd continued, "*I've* got a pranking plan that might put some colour in Mrs Plopwell's cheeks..."

Mr Odd, Edgar and Elsie all creepled off to hide in an airing cupboard, while Mrs Odd prepared a little prank of her own. Within a few minutes, she had joined them again.

"All done, dear?" asked Mr Odd.

"Oh yes," grinned Mrs Odd. "And you'll never guess what Mrs Plopwell's got in her bedside cabinet. A massive pile of wigs! Maybe she's really as bald as a bandicoot, as well as so freakifyingly ugly!"

"What did you do, Mum?" asked Edgar.

"Just you wait and see..." said Mrs Odd.

Moments later, there came a terrific shriek, followed by the sound of a butler loading himself into a catapult and firing himself out of an open window. Mrs Plopwell came tearing out of the bedroom, her face almost unrecognizable under the huge, greasy, hairy green spots that now covered it. She ran into the giant bathroom and began scrubbing her face with a toilet brush.

"Brilliant, Mum," said Edgar, as the Odds peered through a crack in the airing-cupboard door.

"How did you do it?" asked Elsie, filled with awe at her mother's pranking prowess.

Mrs Odd smiled. "I sprinkled a little something into her Vanilla-Cucumber-Avocado-Face Scrub Rejuvenation Cream."

"What, my lovely little lump?" asked Mr Odd.

"Some crushed scorpion stings I found in my pocket. And not just any old crushed scorpion stings, but the stings of the Black Grunting Scorpions of Darkest Peru Where It's So Dark You Can't Even See Your Own Knees."

"Excellent work, my sneaky rat-boiler," said Mr Odd, oozing with pride. "If that won't put the frighteners on 'em, I don't know what will."

Mr Plopwell came sauntering over to the bathroom, his face buried in the paper. "Everything all right, darling?"

"I'm hideous!" screeched Mrs Plopwell.

"Don't be silly, darling," said Mr Plopwell, who

still hadn't looked up. "You're no more hideous now than the day I first met you!"

"That's very sweet of you, dear," said Mrs Plopwell, "but look!" She burst out of the bathroom and showed Mr Plopwell her face in all its huge, greasy, hairy green spotty glory.

"AH!" shrieked Mr Plopwell.

"What?" shrieked Mrs Plopwell.

"Nothing..." gasped Mr Plopwell. "It's just... Look." He showed Mrs Plopwell the paper. "It says here the circus is in town." He shuddered. "You know how I feel about *circuses*. As for your face, well, wait there."

He disappeared into the bedroom and reappeared a few seconds later, both of his hands behind his back. The Odds suddenly had a very queasy uneasy feeling in the bottom of their stomachs. Was another prank about to go wrong?

"What have you got there, dear?" asked Mrs Plopwell, as a particularly large spot on the end of her nose popped.

"Why, the only known cure for huge, greasy, hairy green spots brought on by sudden exposure to the crushed stings of the Black Grunting Scorpions of Darkest Peru Where It's So Dark You Can't Even See Your Own Knees." He held out both of his hands.

"Of course," said Mrs Plopwell. "The saliva of the Spiny Nicaraguan Spitting Lizard!"

Chapter Seven
MR ODD'S CUSTARD TRUCK

"That certainly was lucky, wasn't it, dear?" said Mrs Plopwell, wiping her face clean of the saliva from two Spiny Nicaraguan Spitting Lizards so it was back to its normal hideousness once more.

"Certainly was," Mr Plopwell replied. "And to think I've been after a pair of those tricksy little spitters for my terrarium for years."

"What say now we're dressed," began Mrs Plopwell, "we get another butler from the Plopwell Butler Wardrobe to dress us in our bathing costumes and we take a quick dip in the pool before our meeting with the Mayor?"

"Capital idea, Mrs Plopwell!" said Mr Plopwell. "While we're there we can laugh about all the people that will be left homeless once we demolish that awful Rotten Row."

The Odds watched from their hiding place as the Plopwells toddled off back into the bedroom. Mr Odd produced an already lit candle from the inside pocket of his jacket to illuminate the airing cupboard.

"Well," said Edgar, "that was a lucky coincidence and no mistake."

Mrs Odd looked glum. "I had no idea that Spiny Nicaraguan Spitting Lizard saliva instantly cured huge, greasy, hairy green spots brought on by sudden exposure to the crushed stings of the Black Grunting Scorpions of Darkest Peru Where It's So Dark You Can't Even See Your Own Knees."

"It *is* hard to believe," said Edgar. "And say."

"It was a simple mistake, Mum," said Elsie, patting Mrs Odd's arm. "Anyone could have made it. I'm just sorry we didn't bring our Rare Cartwheeling Jazz Viper eggs instead."

"I used the last of those the other week," said Edgar. "Put them in Eric Hips's lunchbox just before dinnertime. What are you doing, Dad?"

Mr Odd was muttering to himself as he scribbled furiously with a quill pen on the back of a roll of paper.

"Leave him to it," said Mrs Odd. "I've seen your father like this before. He's in the Pranking Zone. And you never disturb a Meddler when they're in the Pranking Zone."

"If I could just ... then perhaps ... through the window ... two crying shepherds and some bubble bath ... sport ... penguin noises..."

Mr Odd's quill was scribbling so quickly it was a blur. After a few more seconds, he stashed the quill and ink back into his jacket and leaped to his feet.

"Right, you lot, this calls for desperate measures. I had a bad feeling about them Plopwells from the start and it's gotten worse."

"What do you mean, Dad?" asked Elsie.

"Meddling legend has it," Mr Odd began, "that spread far and wide throughout the world there are a few, very few, mind, a Chosen Bunch, if you will, that are ... *unprankable*."

The Odds gasped.

THE MEDDLERS' MISCHIEF MANUAL
THE UNPRANKABLE FOE

There may be occasions in a Professional Prankster's career when they will encounter a person or persons who are difficult, perhaps even impossible, to prank. Throughout Meddling history there have been reports of such people, but a Professional Prankster does not give up without a fight. And if it's getting really difficult, just throw a cowpat at them and run away.

"Really?" Edgar whispered.

"Could it be?" Elsie gulped.

"To think I would see this in my lifetime..." said Mrs Odd. "And that it might happen in *my* town, to *my* family!"

"All the signs are there, family of mine," said Mr Odd.

"But what makes someone unprankable, Dad?" asked Elsie.

"No one knows. But I think them

Plopperwellers are two of 'em. They're always one step ahead of you. And when you take that step away, they skip over it anyway and don't even notice it's gone. But we can't be discouraged. They *have* to have a weakness and we *have* to find it. We need to up our game and prank them so well that they run screaming from this house and never return."

"Can't we just throw a cowpat at them?" asked Edgar.

"No, Edgar," said Mrs Odd. "We need them to move out of Trott. A flying cowpat isn't going to do that, is it?"

"But what can we do?" asked Elsie.

"I've got an idea," said Mr Odd. "What is Trott famous for?"

"The Trott Tripwire Test Centre," the others replied.

"Apart from that."

"Nothing."

"Apart from that!"

"Custard?" said Elsie.

"Right you are, Elsie," said Mr Odd. "You three keep an eye on the Plopwells and try to delay their swim for as long as possible. I'll be as quick as I can."

And with that, he disappeared.

"What do you think he's got planned?" asked Elsie.

"Knowing your father, something big," said Mrs Odd.

"Why did Mr Plopwell shudder when he saw the circus was in town?" said Edgar, scratching his head. "Do you think he's scared of circuses?"

"No time for that now, Edgar," said Mrs Odd. "Let's go stall the Plopwells."

Mrs Odd, Edgar and Elsie scrambled out of the airing cupboard and split up, the better to find the Plopwells in their vast mansion.

The Trott Custard Refinery was quite a distance from Choffingly Way in the famous Custard

District of Lower Hump-Nugget, so Mr Odd hopped atop a campervan all along Pillingly Drive, stole a small boy's skateboard to go through Bibbleswicke Gardens, and galloped the rest of the way on a kindly beagle. Spying a large custard truck that had been left unattended by a careless custard-truck driver, Mr Odd slipped inside. He hotwired the engine with his Pocket-Sized Custard-Truck Hotwiring Kit™ and drove off.

Mr Odd arrived with a SCREECH and a SPLOSH back at the Plopwells' house a few minutes later, parking the stolen Trott Custard Refinery custard truck behind a conveniently custard-truck-sized hedge. He produced a spare custard nozzle from his inside pocket, attached it to a pipe and threaded that through a conservatory window. He then proceeded to drain the water from the pool, redirecting it out on to the Plopwells' petunia patch, until the pool was bone dry. Finally, he connected the nozzle and pipe to the truck and filled the pool to the brim with lumpy yellow gloop.

Mr Odd then climbed up to the rafters to get a good view, where he found Mrs Odd and the twins waiting for him.

"We saw you pull up," said Mrs Odd.

"We distracted them for as long as we could, but they're on their way," said Elsie.

"I even threw a cowpat," said Edgar. "But it missed."

At that moment, the Plopwells burst through the door, dressed in their stripy bathing costumes.

"What the..." exclaimed Mr Plopwell.

"Well I..." exclaimed Mrs Plopwell.

The Odds all peered down from the rafters.

"Do you know what this means, dear?" said Mr Plopwell.

"I think I do, dear," said Mrs Plopwell.

The Odds held their breath, waiting to hear the words: *It means we shall have to put our plans to bulldoze Rotten Row and build our Mega-Supermarket on hold until this mess is cleaned up, which could take weeks.*

Instead, what the Odds heard was...

"We finally get to eat the eighteen-foot treacle sponge we bought in Cairo last year!"

The Plopwells rushed off at once to get seven more butlers from the Plopwell Butler Wardrobe to put the sponge into their giant microwave and heat it up, place it in the pool full of custard, and then fetch the Plopwells a pair of giant spoons.

Chapter Eight

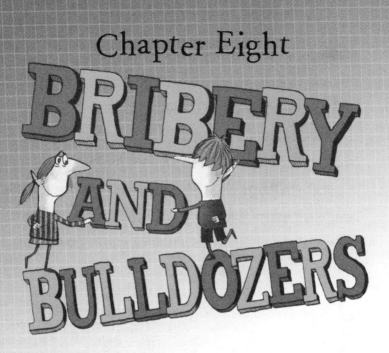

BRIBERY AND BULLDOZERS

For the rest of the morning the Odds watched in bitter defeat as the Plopwells ate twice their body weight in custard, built treacle-castles at the poolside and surfed custard waves on sponge surfboards.

"We haven't even riled them one teeny-tiny bit," said Mr Odd quietly.

"There's *got* to be something else we can try," said Mrs Odd.

"Like what?" asked Elsie. "The custard-swimming-pool prank is one of the biggest Dad's pulled in years. How can we top that?"

Mr Odd didn't like to admit it, but Elsie was right. He wasn't as young as he used to be, and that custard prank had really taken it out of him.

"Oh my!" shrieked Mrs Plopwell, glancing at her rich-person's watch. "Would you look at the time! We'll be late for our meeting with the Mayor!"

"Right you are, dear," said Mr Plopwell, who had just put the finishing touches to a treacle-castle scene, complete with sponge soldiers and a custard moat. "Thank goodness your watch is custard-proof. Totterington!"

The Odds watched helplessly as the Plopwells sauntered from the pool, and got their latest butler to clean and dress them.

"We've got to follow them," said Edgar, as the Plopwells made their way out to their car. "There might still be a chance!"

"What's the point?" said Mr Odd, his hunched shoulders hunching even more.

"We're up against the unprankable," said Mrs Odd. "But that doesn't mean we should give up. What would the Prime Meddler say if he thought we'd given up on a prank?"

"You're right!" cried Mr Odd. "We have a duty to fulfil. Come on, family o' mine, let's be 'avin them Plopperwellers!"

In a flash, the Odds were all piled inside the boot of Mr Plopwell's beloved *Ploppy 1*, zooming down the road towards the town hall.

"What's the plan for when we get there?" asked Elsie.

Mr Odd brought out his candle again so they could all see each other. "Anybody got any ideas?"

"Well..." Edgar began, "there was *one* thing. When Mr Plopwell saw that the circus was in town he sort of ... shuddered."

"You still think he's afraid of circuses?" groaned Elsie.

"Perhaps..." said Edgar.

Just then, *Ploppy 1* screeched to a halt. Mr Odd put his candle back inside his jacket pocket, and the Odds slunk out of the boot and watched the Plopwells march into the town hall.

"What do we do?" asked Elsie. "Follow them?"

"Me and your mother will stay with the Plopsters," said Mr Odd.

"And me and Elsie are going to the circus," said Edgar, grabbing Elsie by the hand.

"I think we've got bigger things to worry about!" said Mrs Odd, as the twins galloped off down the road.

"Leave them to it," said Mr Odd. "We've got to let them plot their own pranks."

Mr and Mrs Odd nipped through the town hall letterbox. They swung across the fancy light fittings high above the Plopwells as the couple were led directly to the Mayor's office, and managed to sneak underneath the grand Mayoral desk just as the huge oak door slammed shut.

"Ah, how lovely of you to come, Mr and Mrs Plopwell," said the Mayor. "Do sit down. Mr Urmston and I have been waiting for you."

"Who's that?" said Mr Odd, pointing at Mr Charles Urmston.

"That's Mr Urmston, Mr Charles Urmston," said Mrs Odd.

"Why is he dressed like somebody's mad auntie?" asked Mr Odd.

"I pranked him yesterday," Mrs Odd grinned. "Maybe he got a taste for wearing dresses."

"Can I get you something to drink?" the Mayor asked the Plopwells. "Tea? Coffee? The tangy juice of the guava?"

"We're fine, Mr Mayor," said Mr Plopwell. "We'd like to get straight down to business, if you don't mind. Mr Urmston?"

Mr Urmston stood up and straightened his tartan dress. "Mr Mayor," he began, "as you know, I'm a businessman. And my business is to make sure that buildings get built. My other business is to make sure other buildings in the way of the buildings I want to build ... shall we say ... *disappear*. Mr and Mrs Plopwell would like to propose a new and exciting project for the town of Trott. One that would re-energize local infrastructure in a failing marketplace with consistent and fluctuating synergy-based reform..."

"What is he on about?" said Mrs Odd, going cross-eyed.

"No idea," said Mr Odd. "But I think he's doing business-people talk. Talk what makes other people so confused that they just agree to whatever you want just so long as you stop talking."

"Well, we need to put a Spaniard in the works before the Mayor grants them permission," said Mrs Odd.

"And before Mr Urmston stops talking," said Mr Odd, gesturing to Mr Urmston, who had now produced a flip chart with lots of squiggly lines and dots and graphs and pie charts.

"Too late!" Mrs Odd said, as Mr Urmston finished his presentation and gave a dainty little curtsy.

The Mayor spoke. "Hmmm," he said. "I'm sorry, Mr and Mrs Plopwell, but I can't let you simply bulldoze Rotten Row just like that. There are laws against such things."

Mr and Mrs Odd grinned like cartoon piranhas.

"Laws?" said Mr Plopwell. "Rumbunkle, says I!"

Mr Odd's mouth fell open in shock. He was about to speak when the Plopwells reached into their pockets and each pulled out a large briefcase stuffed with great thick wads of cash.

"Maybe *this* will change your mind," said Mrs Plopwell.

The Mayor looked at the great thick wads of cash inside the briefcases for two and a quarter seconds, then said, "Do you need me to provide the bulldozers, or do you have your own?"

Chapter Nine
TO PRANK THE UNPRANKABLE FOE

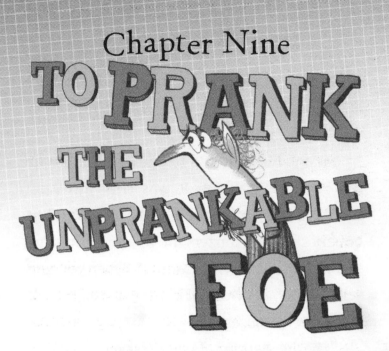

The Plopwells wasted no time in leaving the Mayor's office. Before Mr and Mrs Odd could catch up, they were sitting in *Ploppy 1,* about to head off to Rotten Row.

"No time to get into the boot now, my little gravy-stain," said Mr Odd, as Mr Plopwell revved the engine. "We're gonna have ter cling on for dear life." Mr Odd clamped his spindly fingers round the bumper as Mrs Odd clamped *her* gangling fingers round *his* ankles.

The Plopwells accelerated away with destruction in their hearts, custard in their ears and a couple of Meddlers hanging off the back of their car. Soon they had arrived at Rotten Row.

Mr and Mrs Odd hid underneath the car as the Plopwells got out. It was clear just how confident the Plopwells had been with their bribery skills. Bulldozers, huge cement mixers, steamrollers, enormous cranes and men wearing yellow hard hats were all lined up in front of the bleak row of houses.

"They're starting already?" said Mrs Odd in disbelief. "What about all the people inside?"

"Don't worry about the people inside," Mr Plopwell shouted to Mrs Plopwell. "That's what we've brought the steamrollers for."

The Plopwells tipped back their heads and laughed that horrible, high-pitched cackle once more.

Mr Plopwell turned to one of the steamroller drivers. "In fact, you bog off out of there. *I'll* be the one to start flattening this dump!" The driver got out and scuttled off as the Plopwells' cackling continued.

"Oh, that laugh!" Mrs Odd put her fingers in her ears. "If I hear it one more time..."

Mr Odd's eyes widened. "Wait a minute! That laugh ... those wigs ... rumbunkle... I knew I'd heard it somewhere before!"

But there was no chance to explain, because at that very moment the twins appeared.

"There you are!" said Mrs Odd. "How was the circus?"

"We don't know," said Edgar. "We didn't stay long. Just long enough to arrange a little surprise for Mr Plopwell..."

"Oh yes?" said Mrs Odd.

"It was Edgar's idea," said Elsie. "Mr Plopwell got freaked out before when he knew the circus was in town. And what's the scariest thing at the circus?"

"Elephant poo?" said Mrs Odd. "Overpriced candyfloss?"

"*Clowns!*" said Edgar. "I reckon Mr Plopwell could have a phobia of clowns."

"Brilliant!" said Mrs Odd. "Isn't it, my troubled pimple?" She turned to Mr Odd, but he was nowhere to be seen. "Now where has your father gone?"

"Never mind that. Look!" Edgar pointed to *Ploppy 1*. Mr Plopwell was just about to open the boot to get out his solid-gold hard hat when the boot popped open by itself.

A white-faced, red-nosed, purple-haired clown jumped out. "SURPRISE!" he bellowed, honking his nose as his glittery bowtie spun round.

Mr Plopwell stood there, mouth wide open. "You... you..." he stuttered.

PLOPPY 1

"Oh, you've done it, my little piddlers!" said Mrs Odd. "You found his weakness. If only your father were here to see this."

"Mr Plopwell looks as though he's about to explode!" said Elsie.

She was right. Mr Plopwell was getting redder and redder. "You ... CLOWN!" he roared. "What are you doing inside my *Ploppy 1*? You're spoiling it. Look here, you've got make-up on the interior, not to mention all the stray purple hairs and bowtie glitter! Get OUT!"

The clown tumbled out of *Ploppy 1*. "They said it was your birthday..."

"Well, it's not!" said Mr Plopwell. "Now move away!"

The clown moped off.

"Right!" Mr Plopwell retrieved his golden hard hat and put it on. "Let's get on, shall we? Unless there are any more clowns hidden anywhere?"

He waited a few seconds as another three climbed out of his boot, but Mr Plopwell didn't bat an eyelid.

"He ... he wasn't scared at all," said Edgar.

"We must have been wrong," said Elsie. "He isn't afraid of clowns. He must just dislike circuses."

"The bulldozers are about to start," said Mrs Odd. "Quickly, children, think. There MUST be something else we can do."

"How about we swipe all the keys from the bulldozers and steamrollers?" said Elsie.

"Good idea," said Mrs Odd. "Let's go!"

Mrs Odd and the twins started to sneak off in different directions when Mr Odd appeared. They watched as he marched right up to the Plopwells.

"Wait right there, Plopwells!" Mr Odd said, standing with his hands on his hips, his brown mustard-striped jacket blowing in the breeze like a superhero's cape. "There'll be no bulldozin' or steamrollerin' today!"

"Oh, is that right, you grotty little man?" said Mrs Plopwell. "I think you'll find it's all been signed and approved by the Mayor of Trott himself." She produced a very long and boring-looking contract from inside her handbag.

"That's right," said Mr Plopwell. "It says here that we, Maximillian and Martha Plopwell, have permission to bulldoze Rotten Row and build our own Mega-Supermarket. So there."

"Really?" Mr Odd strode up to Mr Plopwell, strutting like a cocky peacock. He peered at the contract. "Yes, well, that all seems above board. Maximillian and Martha Plopwell *do* have permission to bulldoze Rotten Row..."

"What is he doing?" asked Elsie.

"Just sit back and watch your father at work, children," said Mrs Odd, smiling.

Mr Odd turned and started to walk away. "Oh, there is just *one* thing..." He went back up to Mr and Mrs Plopwell until his pointy nose was touching Mr Plopwell's. "You're not Maximillian and Martha Plopwell. Are you?"

The Plopwells looked at each other for a second and then laughed their insane laugh.

"What a silly little man!" said Mrs Plopwell.

"Quite silly!" said Mr Plopwell. The Plopwells howled again.

"And there it is," said Mr Odd. "That awful laugh... Y'know, I recognize that laugh." The Plopwells stopped laughing. "I used to know a couple, a long time ago, with a laugh almost as horrible as that one. I'd almost forgotten it. But then a few other little clues popped up. You see, in your wardrobe, I'm sure I spotted ... a Stripy-Spit pigeon."

"So?" said Mr Plopwell. "The Stripy-Spit pigeon is a common enough bird!"

"That's right," said Mr Odd. "In Meddleton..."

Mr and Mrs Plopwell looked at each other once more.

"And earlier, my dear wifey spotted a big ol' collection of wigs in your bedside cabinet, Mrs Plopwell..."

"That's right," said Mrs Odd, joining Mr Odd with the twins. "Just what would you need that for, *Mrs Plopwell*?"

"Wigs *are* quite useful things..." Mr Odd stroked his stubbly chin. "...For *disguising* yourself!"

"Go get 'em, my love," Mrs Odd muttered.

"But that wasn't what clinched it for me," said Mr Odd. "Rumbunkle!"

The Plopwells gasped.

"Dad!" said Edgar. "Language!"

"Sorry, Edgar," said Mr Odd. "But there we have it. A Meddler's pet. Wigs. And the use of a Meddling swearword."

"I've heard enough of this nonsense!" said Mr Plopwell, lines of sweat dripping down his face.

"Me too," said Mr Odd. "BOB!"

From behind the Plopwells, the Odds' dog leaped up and with two snaps of his jaws whipped away the Plopwells' wigs to reveal...

"Mr and Mrs Strange!" the Odds cried as one.

The former Plopwells stood there, mouths agape. Mr Strange, with his beady, shifty little eyes and pointy Meddler ears and nose, and Mrs Strange, her lank and greasy hair down to her shoulders.

"Mr and Mrs Strange..." said Mrs Odd. "Meddlers trying to prank other Meddlers out of their own homes. For shame..."

"You mean the Stranges wanted us out of our house, so they set this whole thing up?" said Elsie.

"That's right," said Mr Odd. "And as *The Meddlers' Mischief Manual* says... Edgar?"

"'Never nick from other nickers,'" said Edgar.

"That's a Meddling law!" Mr Odd pointed a finger at the Stranges. "And I've just called the COPs..."

"The cops?" said Mr Strange. "HA! No prison cell can hold the Stranges!"

"Sorry!" Mr Odd smacked his forehead. "What was I thinking? I meant the Council of Prankification. I just put an 's' on the end."

The Stranges looked at each other in horror.

"All right, Odds," said Mrs Strange. "You've found us out. We wanted to live in Rotten Row so we pretended to be the Plopwells. We made sure it got into the paper that we'd moved into Snootypants Manor because we knew Mr Odd wouldn't be able to resist poking his nose in."

"So they knew we were watching them the

whole time?" said Elsie. "That's why we thought they were unprankable! They have Meddlers' minds, so they were expecting everything we did!"

"That's right!" said Mr Strange.

"And we would've got away with it too, if it hadn't been for you meddling Odds!"

"Well, I'm not waiting around here to be arrested and thrown into *Meddler* prison," said Mrs Strange, jumping into *Ploppy 1*.

"Me neither," said Mr Strange, jumping in after her. "See you around, suckers!" Mr Strange bellowed, as he fumbled with his car keys.

"What are you fumbling for, you pimple-faced pustule!" said Mrs Strange. "Let's get out of here!"

"My key!" said Mr Strange. "It won't work!"

"Earwax," Mr Odd smiled. "My own special recipe. Clogged up your ignition good and proper."

The Odds laughed.

"BOB!" Mr Odd yelled.

A very loud and extremely irritating beeping sound began, as if some large and extremely irritating vehicle was backing up. Everyone turned to see that it was coming from a cement-truck, which was reversing very slowly towards *Ploppy 1*. Now it has to be said that Bob the Odd's dog could not do many things well. Things that normal dogs do, anyway. He rarely sat when he was told to, he didn't play dead, beg for food or shake paws. However, manocuvring and operating a ten-ton cement mixer came quite naturally to him.

"Now look here!" said Mr Strange. "Let's talk about this, shall we? It was just a prank. A PRANK!"

With a wag of his tail, Bob dumped the entire contents of the cement truck all over *Ploppy 1* and the Stranges.

The Odds hugged each other as the cement dried, instantly trapping those terrible tricksters.

"We'll be back!" Mrs Strange screeched, as the wail of Meddler sirens were heard in the distance. "You wait and see!"

Mr Odd grinned. "It was a nice try, Stranges. But no one beats the Odds!"

Chapter Ten

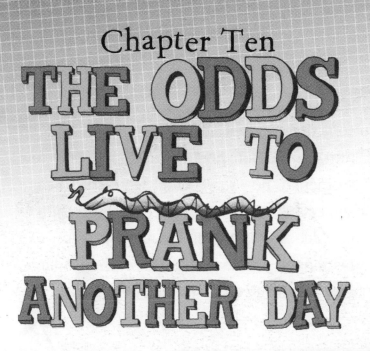

THE ODDS LIVE TO PRANK ANOTHER DAY

The next morning, Bob the Odd's dog was given pride of place smack-dab in the centre of the breakfast table, instead of under it. Mr Odd had even given Bob his and Mrs Odd's duvet to sleep on (it was covered in fleas anyway).

The rest of Rotten Row never really knew just how close they had come to getting squished by steamrollers. But the Odds, at least, were safe in the knowledge that even though Bob was getting on in years, he could still prank with the best of them.

"Yep," said Mr Odd, as he heaped a sugary spoonful of porridge into his mouth, "that'll be something to tell the grandkiddlers and no mistake. Old Bob, here..." he stopped. For a few moments he sat completely still before somersaulting from his chair and spitting porridge all over the dining room. He stuck out his tongue, which was now covered in large, greasy, hairy green spots. "You two!" he grinned.

"We thought you'd appreciate that, Dad!" sniggered Edgar. "Crushed stings from the Black Grunting Scorpions of Darkest Peru Where It's So Dark You Can't Even See Your Own Knees!"

"We found an extra packet in my sock drawer! A nice little everything's-back-to-normal prank," chuckled Elsie.

Just then, there came a familiar shriek from the kitchen. Mrs Odd came careening into the dining room.

"What's the matter, dear?" asked Mr Odd, still spitting out globules of hairy porridge.

But his question was answered by the two Rare Cartwheeling Jazz Vipers, which rolled out of the kitchen hissing with glee.

"That's the last of the eggs," Edgar roared.

"Promise!" snorted Elsie.

The Odds all got up from their chairs and chased the Rare Cartwheeling Jazz Vipers upstairs and all around the house until finally they managed to lock them in the twins' bedroom.

Laughing and panting breathlessly, they trooped back downstairs to the breakfast table. But before they all sat down, Mr Odd raised a glass of nettle juice in a toast and said, "To Bob, the finest dog a Meddler family could have!"

"TO BOB!" the rest of the Odds cried in unison. They all took a swig of their nettle juice before sitting down heavily on their chairs...

...which all promptly broke, sending the Odds crashing to the floor in a mess of splinters, hairy porridge, cutlery and nettle juice.

From his new position in the centre of the breakfast table, Bob gave a wheezy laugh as he held up a familiar-looking rusty old saw.

TEST QUESTIONS FROM THE SOCIETY OF MEDDLERS' PROFESSIONAL PRANKSTER EXAM

Do you have what it takes to be a Professional Prankster, or are you merely a Trainee Trickster? Take the test and find out!

1. You see a man walking towards you carrying a very large and expensive-looking cake. Do you:
A. Offer to give him a hand – it looks heavy and awkward.
B. Tickle the man under his arms.
C. Wait until he's near a very smartly dressed person and then trip him up.

2. What is the fewest number of pockets Meddlers (Professional Prankster and Trainee Trickster alike) are expected to have about their person?
A. Two. Nice and normal.
B. One, as long as it's full of Mischief-Making tricks.
C. Seventeen.

3. Which of the following is expected to be found in a Meddler's pocket?

A. Sweets and kittens for the less fortunate.

B. Something that might give a fright, but nothing living, though — ewww!

C. At least the following: live earthworms, slugs or other slimy invertebrates, itching powder or the crushed stings of the Black Grunting Scorpions of Darkest Peru Where It's So Dark You Can't Even See Your Own Knees, spare pants (elasticated), custard (or similar), one spare Custard Nozzle, eggs (any kind), a live shrew called Benjamin.

4. Give the definition (as stated in *The Meddlers' Mischief Manual*) of the verb "to slope".

A. What?

B. To slope is to push someone very fast down a ski run, if possible while they're not wearing skis.

C. Sloping is a bit like skulking, only slopier.

5. Why should one (Meddler or otherwise) never nick from other nickers?

A. Because it's not nice to nick.

B. You should! What's wrong with that?

C. Because it is against Meddling law and could very well end with you being covered in cement and carted off by the Council of Prankification.

RESULTS

MAINLY As – Commiserations. You do not have what it takes to be a Professional Prankster. I doubt you'd even make a passable Trainee Trickster. In fact, you're probably not even a Meddler at all, are you? Admit it!

MAINLY Bs – Well done. You would make a very adequate Trainee Trickster. With the correct training and pockets full of pranks you could, one day, be well on your way to Professional Pranksterdom.

MAINLY Cs – CONGRATULATIONS! You are, clearly, already a Professional Prankster. You take opportunities to prank whenever you can and there is very little left to teach you. You must, from now on, be your own teacher and push yourself ever onwards to new heights of prankery. WELL DONE!